I Am Small

For Lou

This edition published by Kids Can Press in 2018

First edition 2018.
Originally published in French under the title *Je suis petite*
by Comme des géants inc.

Published with the permission of Comme des géants inc.,
CP 65006 BP Mozart, Montreal, Quebec, Canada H2S 0A3

Translation rights arranged through VeroK Agency, Barcelona, Spain

Kids Can Press gratefully acknowledges the financial support of the Government of Ontario, through the Ontario Media Development Corporation; the Ontario Arts Council; the Canada Council for the Arts; and the Government of Canada, through the CBF, for our publishing activity.

Published in Canada and the U.S. by Kids Can Press Ltd.
25 Dockside Drive, Toronto, ON M5A 0B5

Kids Can Press is a Corus Entertainment Inc. company

www.kidscanpress.com

The artwork in this book was rendered in pen and ink and watercolor.
The text is set in Georgia.

Original edition edited by Nadine Robert and Mathieu Lavoie
English edition edited by Yvette Ghione
Designed by Mathieu Lavoie

Printed and bound in Shenzhen, China, in 3/2018 by C & C Offset

CM 18 0 9 8 7 6 5 4 3 2 1

Library and Archives Canada Cataloguing in Publication

Leng, Qin
[Je suis petite. English]
I am small / by Qin Leng.

Translation of: Je suis petite.
ISBN 978-1-5253-0115-5 (hardcover)

I. Title. II. Title: Je suis petite. English.

PS8623.E579J413 2018 jC843'.6 C2018-900764-8

Qin Leng

I Am Small

Kids Can Press

My name is Mimi.

I am very small.

I might as well be called Mini.

It's true!

At home, Daddy, Mommy, Nicholas and Marie are all taller than me.

So is Gus, our dog!

It’s the same thing at school.

All my friends tower over me.

And sidewalk crowds are the worst!

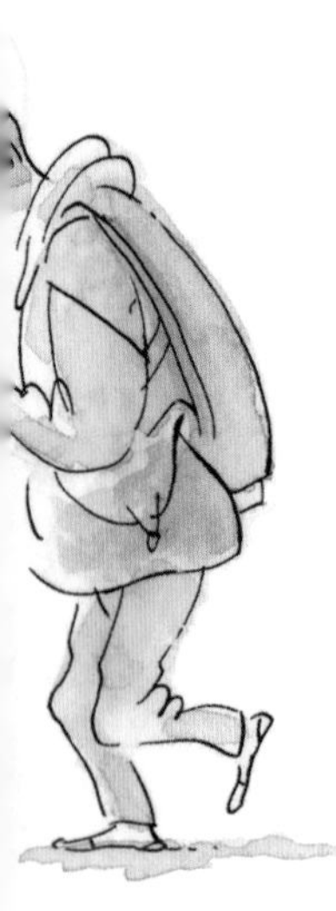

I wouldn't be surprised if nobody noticed me.

Being small really bugs me.

When will I grow big enough to take up as much space in the world as everyone else?

SPINAC
to grow big and strong

My feet barely reach the edge of the seat on the bus.
I bounce all over the place on the way to school.

At Olivia's bakery, I can't even see all the pretty desserts in the display case.

Just imagine the trouble I have picking the nicest cake!

At Pete's butcher shop, the sausage links are longer than me! (I checked.)

At Jack's fish market, the catch of the day stares at me with its big bulgy eyes, ready to swallow me up in one gulp.

And in class, I can only reach the bottom of the blackboard.
It's annoying, especially when I have a lot I want to write.

"Why are you complaining?" Remy asked me the other day. "You're always first in the cafeteria line and you get the biggest piece of cake.

"When I try to hurry to the front of the line, I end up bumping into everyone," he said.

“You always win at hide-and-seek!” Annie told me later. “I wish I could squeeze into small hiding places like you can. I’m always the first to be found.”

“And you’re always in the front row for class pictures,” Celeste added. “I have to stand in the back, even when I wear my favorite shirt, the one with the funny yeti. You can only see my head.”

At home, Nicholas said, “I envy all your small secret places.

“Mine always get in someone's way in the kitchen or in the living room.”

But they just don't get it!

I'm frustrated because they can do a lot of stuff that I can't, because I'm so small.

Isn't it obvious?!

But ... well ... if I think about it, it's possible that there are some advantages to being small.

Like snuggling in bed between Mommy and Daddy ...
Or playing Knights with Gus ...

Or practicing for the synchronized swimming championship in the bathtub (my pretend pool).

One day after school,
Daddy comes to get me.
He's all bright-eyed and smiley

“There’s a surprise at home,” he tells me.
A surprise? I love surprises!
What could it be?

A real-life swimming pool?

A hot-air balloon?

The biggest piece of cake in the world?

When we get home, I throw my bag on the floor
and run to my room ...

“The surprise is in here,” Daddy says, pointing to his and Mommy’s bedroom.

At first, I don't notice anything.

Then I see him.

All pink, and a little wrinkled like me when I stay in the bathtub too long.

“Meet Max, your little brother,” whispers Mommy.
“He’s super small!” I say.

“Of course. He’s brand new,” Mommy says. “You started out like this, too, you know. Very small! And look at you now — a big sister.”

Mommy's right.

So, whispering carefully because Max's ears are also very small, I tell him, "Just be patient. One day you'll be big, too!"